I0521486

Storylandia

The Wapshott Journal of Fiction

Issue 30

Storylandia, Issue 30, The Wapshott Journal of Fiction, ISSN 1947-5349, ISBN 978-1-942007-25-8 is published at intervals by the Wapshott Press, now a 501(c)(3) nonprofit, PO Box 31513, Los Angeles, California, 90031-0513, telephone 323-201-7147. All correspondence can be sent to The Wapshott Press, PO Box 31513, LA CA 90031-0513. Visit our website at www.WapshottPress.org to learn more. This work is copyright © 2019 by Storylandia. The Wapshott Journal of Fiction, Los Angeles, California. Copyright © 2018 George Gad Economou and is reprinted here with the copyright owner's permission.

Storylandia is always seeking quality original short stories, novelettes, and novellas. Please have a look at our submission guidelines at www.Storylandia.WapshottPress.org or email the editor at editor@wapshottpress.org

Donations happily accepted at donate.wapshottpress.org

Cover image by Lauren Matulac

Storylandia

The Wapshott Journal of Fiction

Founded in 2009

Issue 30, Summer 2019

Edited by Ginger Mayerson

Letters to S.

By George Gad Economou

Letters to S.

by
George Gad Economou

Letters to S.

28/08/2014
(unsent)

Everywhere I look there they are, a set of black eyes staring at me from every corner, from every possible direction. Even when I close my own eyes they're still there, amid the darkness of my closed eyelids, staring intensely, curiously, admiringly. They have a gleam, a shining I have never before seen; they're both scary and comforting.

It feels good seeing them staring at me with that intention of theirs, and yet it makes me uncomfortable, because it scares me; what do they want—I wonder often silently—what do they expect of me? There is no certain answer—I can't tell why the look is there.

I know why the eyes are following me—that's a simple question that needs not be asked. Yet, what do they want from me, I do not know. I have my own hopes about it, I wish and pray for a specific answer to be true, but I can't possibly know.

Three days I've been followed by this particular set of eyes; the knowledge of seeing them again in person, *in vivo*, is exhilarating, yet scary. I need to know what they want, what the thoughts that make the gleam appear are, why they seemingly shine whenever they meet my own glance. What is it? I ask myself, but no one comes to the rescue, the answer is seemingly non-existent.

It isn't so, and I know it well—there is an answer to the question tormenting my mind, a very definitive answer. Yet, the struggle is to obtain it—there are feasible ways, yet the plausibility of acquiring an unwanted answer is high. Am I willing, then, to risk everything and ask the burning question? I have no answer to that, either.

And maybe it's this last question that does the tormenting; the uncertainty of the future and the uncertainty of my own mind on whether it will survive the unexpected answer—whether the reason behind the shining black eyes that open widely whenever they meet mine is vastly different than what I hope.

I am not the first, nor will I be the last, to be tormented by such questions and by the vast uncertainty that lies within those situations—yet, whensoever you find yourself in such a peculiar situation—for the details of my current condition are more complicated and bizarre than I had led you, my dear reader, to believe—you suddenly lose your mind, your capability of socializing properly. Perhaps it's purely biological; different hormones are produced in the mind when there's real interest, and not just superficial attraction, which, therefore, makes the approach different, and tougher. For it's for more that I hope and wait and pray, yet will it come?

Or will this hesitation, the reluctance derived from the fear of the unknown, prove to be fatal? Will I be followed by those eyes forever only in my dreams, or will I, at some point, be able to stare into them at will, and in person? More questions arise in my mind, while I struggle to answer even the simplest one.

I know what needs be done—I've done it a lot of times in my turbulent past, and I'm certain I shall do it again in the future. Yet, what if those black eyes—that are now staring at me through the paper upon which I type—are meant to be something more? A life-changing moment? From when I first laid my eyes upon them, from that very first exchange of glances, there was something... a sparkling, if we're to use common terminology.

I saw it in the eyes and felt it appear in mine too —a good sign, I know. Yet, is the fear of not knowing what the eyes—or, to put it better, their owner—want and feel, or is the fear inside me, that renders me incapable of trying to seek for the answers?

And, as it always happen, it's the last question that proves to be the most important, instantaneously rendering all previous questions worthless.

And therefore, I now find myself questioning myself: what do I want? Isn't that, after all, the biggest question, the main issue? I know what the eyes want, or at least I'm quite certain of it. I've seen the gleam before, I've seen the right movements being made. I am confident in knowing the answers to my previous questions.

Is it, thus, because of my uncertainty regarding my own feelings that I try to make these questions unanswerable? Probably yes. It's me, after all and not some general uncertainty, that obliterates the answers, that makes the simplest of questions tough and unanswerable. Therefore, what needs be done, apparently, is for me to seek the answer inside my mind, for it's there that it lies, and not in some strange, exotic place: what do I want?

Is there really an answer, though? I want to continue my life as it always was, regardless of how turbulent, crazy, unstable it may be; yet, a part of me needs a change, and preferably a drastic one. Hence, do I take my chances? Do I attempt to bring the black eyes, and their owner, into my life, possibly for good?

Am I willing to let my past be past, and look into the future? Am I really seeking a future vastly different than my past and present? And if yes, will I be able to keep this promise, namely to stay, forever and ever, a changed person? Or will I take the chance, ruin it, revert back to my old self, and consequently bring tears in those dark eyes?

Questions, questions, questions... yet, where are the answers? Are there any answers? Yes, they are inside me; but I have to search deep, dig way deep down in my mind, in order to find them. And, the most important aspect of it all, I don't know if I dare look—I am terrified of what I may discover.

26/09/2014
(sent while stoned)

My dearest S–,

Where do I begin, how do I... I guess it's only fair to start from the beginning, explain the reasons why I write this... will you ever see it, I wonder silently, uncertain.

But, whether you'll see it or not, doesn't really matter to me... all I need right now is this moment with my thoughts, to see how I really feel. So... where do I begin?

Well, from the get-go, from when I first met you, there was the attraction, the sexual tension, or whatever you may want to call it. We both felt it and, because of the honesty that characterizes this relationship, we both knew it, too.

I did understand, quite quickly I must admit, that there was something wrong, that you weren't readily available; I just sensed that *something* was holding you back. I didn't quite catch it at first, but I think I can be excused for that, considering how utterly complicated the entire situation was, and, I guess, still is. Nevertheless, I knew the complexity, it was entirely voluntarily that I decided to bring myself into this whole fucking mess; you didn't drag me into it, so there's absolutely no reason for you to feel guilty, for *anything*.

What I don't think, however, you understand, is how much you came to mean to me during this month, or so, we've known each other; I know I often joke about it and make some of the most serious things I say to you seem like nothing but bad jokes. I do this, possibly because I've never had to express my feelings before in my life—mostly because I never had such feelings for anyone.

You've changed my whole life, my mindset, my... you changed *me*. And, in all honesty, I don't even know if I can take it. What do I mean? That you've asked me to change a lot about myself, I made promises I *never* make, and intend to keep them too, yet, even though I know you asked those changes because you care for me, I don't know for how long I will accept those very changes, when I know that...

That what? I guess, the right answer, at least for me, is until I know there's a chance you'll be mine; something which I now know will never happen. "Beautiful to dream", was your own words to describe the prospect of us being together—yet, you prefer staying with your current boyfriend, for whatever fucking reasons you may have, which I don't understand. For me, your reasoning sounds like pure motherfucking bullshit, but, probably, that's because your mindset is totally alien to me—similarly, my own mindset and how I think must seem like utter motherfucking bullshit to you.

Sorry for the vulgarity, I slip up sometimes—yet, no reason to erase anything. You shall probably never read this, anyhow. And, if you do, it will probably be because I'm finally dead; in that case, feel free to visit my tombstone and complain about the swearing!

At any rate, the fact is, I can't help but think of the pointlessness of this entire fucking charade. I mean, you're not going to break up with your boyfriend—you're too caught up in your whole "one and only" kind of thinking to ever grow the balls to do it; the only way you'd do such thing, would be if he cheated on you, or broke up with you explicitly, and, in my honest opinion, he seemed too "caring" to ever do so (I had a whole different word in mind, mind you!)—and we both know it. Yet, I still insist on hoping. Why?

I'm asking myself the same damn thing. Why? Why in all that's fucking holy am I still insisting that there's a chance? I mean, truly, I do believe you may be my only chance for happiness, perhaps it's therefore I still pursue that vague, dead dream, and yet, I know there's no chance. I know, too damn fucking well, that I'm never going to be happy. Possibly, I need to be miserable, depressed, sad, and all those other wonderful things, in order to be a productive writer—maybe I secretly seek out misery and melancholy. It could well be the main reason I've never had a serious relationship; I'm afraid happiness will kill my writing talent.

And still, I'm willing to put even my fucking talent, the only thing I'm good at and the only thing I cherish in this entire fucking world, at such a great risk, just so I can be with you. Should I ever tell these things to you? That's an answer you'll have to give me, when I'm dead. Just whisper it at the tombstone—maybe, a part of my soul will somehow evade the deepest pits of Hell; or whatever comes in the afterlife.

And now you can see why I'd never give you

this letter while I was still alive. How would you react if you realized that I'm having another major depressive episode because of you? Because of the whole damn fucking situation? I don't enjoy anything; even writing, at times, seems a dull task. I find no pleasure in anything—and yet, just a few days ago, I was happier than I've ever been. What changed?

You decided we should only meet in public places; no more you visiting my apartment. And yes, I understand your reasons—I don't agree with them, I personally think they're the most idiotic excuses I've ever heard in my life (and trust me, I've both heard and said a lot of stupid, idiotic, moronic, plain out dumb excuses), but I can see the reasoning, because I'm beginning to understand the crazy way of your thinking.

Needless to say, how could I ever tell you these things? I would never emotionally blackmail you to come to my place; it's not your fault that I'm so emotionally unstable that I got depressed, when I realized I would never properly hug you again. Maybe I should have kissed you when I had the chance— maybe that would have changed your mind, maybe that would have given me some chances of ending up with you. As we now stand—since I decided to keep my promises, for the first time in my miserable life—I guess I have to accept the fact I'll only see you in public places, our touching will be minimized to a hug goodbye, and soon, when things will get better with your boyfriend, you'll start avoiding me altogether, afraid that the still existing sexual attraction will be too much for you to bear. You thought it cheating when we held hands; soon, you'll think you're cheating on him, simply because you may think of me sometimes.

Well, it may be for the best; you go back to

him, devote your time to being happy with him, and I'm sure you'll soon forget all about me. I'll be a vague memory, a faint shade of the past. You'll recall me every once in a while, hopefully you'll smile faintly at the memories of what transpired between us, then you'll return to your life—which I sincerely hope will be a long and happy one.

As for me? Well, I'll get over you, I'll start drinking again, I'll start partying again, I'll start womanizing again. I'll return to the empty shell of my former life; no emotions, no love, no compassion, no one to care for, and no one to care for me. I'll do whatever the fuck I want, I'll have no one to tell me to take better care of my health. I'll go back to fucking every hot piece of ass that happens to smile at me, I'll return to drinking one bottle of bourbon daily, and I'll continue writing—the only difference will be that I'll know I am capable of loving and caring and all that bullshit, but I'll refuse to let anyone else know.

Only you got a glimpse of that side of myself, the loving part, and you shall remain the only, too. Not because I'm afraid to give it to someone else—seems familiar?!—but simply because I am certain I'll never find anyone else worthy of it. The world is a fucked up place. You got your "only one"; or so I hope, for otherwise you'll be devastated.

Maybe I got my "only one" too, in a different sense, but, in my case, I lost her. I wasted my only chance in happiness, and, maybe, I'm glad about it. At least now, I can focus entirely on my writing. Guess I have to look at the bright side of life.

I suppose you can now understand why I would never say such things to you; why I couldn't utter these harsh words. Probably, if you're reading this, you'll think it's your fault, that you drove me back to a lifestyle that led to my inevitable death. It's *not* your fault. I was born a fault, a failure. You had nothing to do with my demise, with my depression, with my death.

You're more innocent than I was at the age of 7; and, in order to conclude this with something true, I find this admirable and I'm actually glad I wasn't given the chance to spoil you. Perhaps, for your sake, it is better if we part ways—I suppose, though, since you're reading this, we've already parted ways.

> *Will remember you forever with nothing but love,*
> *G-*

> *03/10/2014*
> *(sent while drunk)*

The moments are what we live for; one kiss, one glance, one... moments of greatness and ultimate happiness. That's all that matters, what makes this fucking world go round. Yet, these moments are but that, moments. All the dreams, hopes, wishes and all that accompany them, all that they promise, last only for a moment, a brief second.

When the second is gone, so are the promises, the dreams, the desires; moments are thus nothing but that, moments. When they're done, misery, melancholy, pain and tears come—is there, thus, a point in living? What's the meaning of life, if happiness cannot last?

One kiss is a moment of great happiness, especially with someone special, someone important, that certain someone you hold closest to your heart, the person you can see yourself growing old with. When the kiss is done, and the person is gone, *forever*, how can you *not* return to the oblivion of alcohol and drugs? How can anyone say that life's worth living, when all it gives you is disappointment with pain? How much more can one take, before they say "screw this shit, I'm out" and decide to blow their brains out, just to put an end to a never-ending misery?

Hope; that's the only solution, the only thing that keeps us alive and fighting. Hope for something new, something... a new moment, a new second, a new dose of happiness. Like junkies, we fight and struggle until the next dose of happiness—we live and breathe and fight through the, often unbearable, pain, just with the hope of the next moment.

Yet, hope is taken away sometimes. "No hope," and it's all over; the moment's gone, the hope's gone. What's left, then?

Nothing. Yet, we still survive, still going after the damn next moment, that we know will never come— yet we pray, dream, wish, desire with all of our heart that it will, that a next moment is brewed somewhere, awaiting us for when we reach the bottom. Then it comes, it brings us right back up on the top—then the moment's gone and the circle starts all over again.

Even with hope utterly shattered, completely destroyed, with all our dreams turned into small piles of ashes, we still survive, making ourselves—forcing ourselves—to believe in a hope that is dead. We want to believe in resurrection, that hope can somehow come back from the dead; it can't, it will remain dead *forever*, and we know it, yet we believe.

We are stupid for believing a dead hope will come back, but we have to believe so nonetheless, otherwise, death is the only solution. In the dilemma between a resurrected hope and our own perishing, we choose hope simply because we're afraid of death even more so than we're afraid of the pain of the never-resurrected hope.

Pointless existences, meaningless compromises, endless sacrifices: that's Life. We suffer, just so we can enjoy the moments. The moments are gone, the suffering never ends.

Yet the memories of the moments live on, and, maybe, that's the point, after all; being able to recollect the moments you cherish, and see them as bright lights in an otherwise dark existence; the bright lights at the end of the tunnel. We live for the moments, and the memories, and we try to ignore the pain. Maybe, that's the meaning of Life; to brighten up the tunnel of Death.

12/10/2014
(written while high on blow; sent while drunk)

What's the easy way out? Is it easy to accept what life gives you? Isn't there a saying that says "when life gives you lemons, make lemonade"? Am I, thus, supposed to take the hard way, when *some* things are easy in my life? Am I supposed to make my life even harder than it already is?

I've tried many times to do the right thing, although I always hate talking about it; I prefer talking about the times I did the wrong thing, simply because the stories are funnier, and the melancholy feelings are not so overwhelming. I try to look at the bright side, otherwise I shall pull the trigger. I try to keep a positive outlook at everything, otherwise, there's no way out but Death. Is Death the easy way out? In a sense, yes. So, once again, I'm doing the easy thing. Yet, when living is so unbearable, why shouldn't I do the only easy thing?

When life's so damn tough, when everything I do is wrong, when everything I say is wrong, when the fact I was born was a great wrong, *why* shouldn't I, for once, take the easy way out?

I am crazy enough as it is; why should I deliberately add to this by putting even more pressure on myself, just because things have to be done the hard way? People say "don't kill yourself, you still are worth something". Well, I'm worth nothing; I'm worth nothing as a writer, as a friend, as a son, as a human being. I'm a total failure—yet, I'm still alive, still trying to do the right thing, even if I'm seemingly incapable of it. Is this, thus, truly the easy way out? I haven't pulled the trigger yet, no matter how tempting it is, I didn't jump in front of the oncoming traffic—a chance to take the easy way out was presented to me so generously, yet I refused it. Why?

I know what I want in life, I've always pursued it—however, I don't know how to get it, because of who, and what, I am. I know what I want, and it's not my current life—yet, when you are like me, you have to take whatever you can, because you know one day the trigger *will* be pulled. Am I wrong in not always doing the right thing, for sometimes choosing the easy way?

Perhaps, yes. Definitely, you think so; I don't really blame you, because I know you can't understand me, as I can't understand you. You don't know how it is to live in my head, how it is to have numerous voices speaking to you constantly; I don't know how it is to live with your kind of pressure.

Therefore, we're both wrong when we try to advise each other; however, I only meant to help. Perhaps you reacted negatively because of what I said—in which case, I honestly apologize. Yet, I know we shall never be together, in whatever sense, simply because I am what I am. Regardless of what I want, of what I often dream, I know you'll never be there for me, because I always say and do the wrong things.

Stupid jokes; impossible, harsh advice; strong words with honest feelings and emotions, which you can't believe as true—yes, that's me, always has been. I may wear a different mask, when I'm around others, but you get the true picture. Believe it or not, I don't care any longer. You may believe I try to play you—perhaps it is for the best too, because it will make some things easier for you. But, I know, I adamantly *know*, I'm the real me around you; unfortunately, only around you.

And that's because I hate my real self, I loathe the son of a bitch that can ruin everything in seconds. Yet, I felt the need to be myself, because I cared for you, because I needed you to see the real me, for whatever reasons I might have had at the time.

Maybe because I cared so much for you, I didn't want to deceive you—maybe because I felt that you cared for me, too, so I didn't want to give you a wrong impression. No matter the reason, I've always been myself around you, yet that does not mean you can understand the Hell that's going on inside my mind. Hell, *I* can't understand it and I'm living it daily.

So, when I take the easy way, when I try to avoid the hard things, I succeed, and it's the only time I feel some happiness, some kind of accomplishment. When I try to do the hard, and often right, thing, I fail miserably, and I end up wishing to pull the trigger—just like I feel now, and for the past few weeks.

In conclusion, I don't know why I wrote you this—perhaps because I felt pissed off for some reason, and wanted to clarify something. Mostly, however, because I finally realized you were missing a big part of the puzzle that is me. I never reveal things, even to those I care for the most (that small group involves you too), so I couldn't do that to you, to invite you into my Hell. But now, since I fear I may lose you, I had to say it. I mentioned I'm manic-depressive, yet I never truly explained what it means. You can always google "Type II bipolar disorder", but I doubt you'll find a good explanation of what it is to be inside the mind of such an insane person... so, *fuck off*!

13/10/2014

I want to apologize for how I was today, for how I talked, for the way I looked; unfortunately, I can't help it, nor can I stop myself from thinking. I have a lot of things on my mind at the moment, but, unfortunately—mostly for *you*—what I think most about *is* you, and all the things that transpired during the month and a half we've known each other.

Yes, I do care about you; yes, I do value our friendship; yes, I do *not*, under any circumstances, want to lose you; yes, I have strong feelings for you; and yes, I know you once *had* similar, albeit I doubt as strong, feelings for me, which are now diminishing, if they have not vanished altogether.

I also know—and I *have* mentioned it once or twice—that the time you spend with me depends on how things are going with your other part of your life, the most important one. I realize I'm not important, or at least not in the same sense; I doubt I can live with it, but I must learn to cope with it—hopefully, one day I'll come to that. What I had, however, mentioned, and what possibly made me so miserable today, was that I know that the time we spend together depends on that other part of your life.

When you didn't want to go home, when things were going bad, you would spend most of your time with me—that's when I began caring for you. You needed me, I needed you too. The first time we went out, we stayed together for I don't know how many hours; you mentioned you didn't want to go home. During the big *fredagsbar*, we prolonged our staying together for up until it got too late. The first times at my place, you took one of the last busses—during the next visits, you had to go away sooner, now you've stopped visiting altogether. Soon, we'll meet for a quick coffee, exchange some brief news, then you'll be on your way home. You're busy, too, I know *that*, but I highly doubt it's the only reason we can't be together for long. As things get better in your life, you'll see me less and less, because you'll *want* to go home and not because you *have* to. It's perfectly understandable— you don't experience the misery I do—yet I can't help but feel miserable, when I know all too well that soon we'll barely see each other; once, you thought you were cheating by being at my place and holding my hand—at some point, even seeing me will feel like cheating. I wrote that already somewhere, but the fact of the matter is you know how I feel, and I doubt you've managed to eliminate your feelings towards me altogether, although I'm certain you've tried.

You said "beautiful to dream", when things looked bad; you said "no hope", when things were better. You kissed me, because you wanted to show me I'm important, but you also did so, because you wanted to say goodbye; to take it out of your system, in order to allow things to get better. You wanted to let it go, you did it because you wanted to say goodbye.

I don't want to say goodbye—I know, sometimes

it's the only way, but it's tough to do so—and I think, and hope, you don't want to either. You want me to move on, because that way I'll be out of the equation. I want to move on, because I know I'm not in the equation; the toothbrush, the "beautiful to dream", everything that happened during this time, were things you did, because you feared for the future. You were in a bad place, and maybe you saw a way out in me; now, since things have gotten definitely better, you wish to erase it all, to erase whatever you might have felt for me, and fix your life. In all sincerity, I wish you do, especially if it's what it takes to make you happy—besides, my happiness is insignificant, unimportant. I was never happy, nor will I ever be... that's another story.

However, what I can't stop thinking about, what kills me, is that the better things go for you, the more I won't see you; it's killing me. Just as much as it kills me knowing that I cannot say "I need you", because you won't be able to come. You can't, nor do you want to, come to my place to hold my hand when I feel like shit, because it may awake the feelings you've put to sleep. Yet, I sometimes *need* you to hold my hand; that's why I keep asking about the tea-box; I need to know that one day, you may come back, even if just as a friend. I know it'll never happen, yet you insist I should keep it. It's killing me, too.

Maybe one day the feelings will die—everything dies eventually, after all—and then things will be different. The problem is, when that day comes, you may not want to be around me anymore—things will be good in your life for you to need me, *or*, I will just have reverted back to my old self, whom you won't like.

This is *not* a goodbye letter, nor a way to pressure you into making a decision. All it is, appearances to the contrary notwithstanding, is a plain explanation of *why* I am the way I am during the past few days (and why I've felt like shit for the past few weeks). It's getting worse, because it's obvious things are getting better and you're proving me right: you're not altogether avoiding me, but you *are* trying to avoid spending too much time with me, or enacting any moment that could be termed even remotely intimate: we held hands on Thursday and you hated it, even though I needed you to do so, just because I had to feel a caring touch; you hated the prolonged hugs of Wednesday night. Whenever we are too close, it awakens feelings within you and you wish them away. I can't help it; I don't do these things because I want to make you choose something you don't want to. I do them because that's me *and* because it's what I need.

I think the main problem is that we met during a time we both needed someone in our lives to care for, and whom would care for us. We found each other—for which I'm extremely glad—yet, the problem is, you have someone else too. You were afraid you'd lose him, so you held onto me tight; now, you're certain you'll fix the problems, so I'm not so needed any longer. It makes sense, too. You chose him, amongst other reasons, so that you'd have someone to comfort you.

I, on the other hand, have no one; nor do I want anyone else. I tried the caring business once or twice, and I always end up hurt—I'll never stop caring about you, but I'll never move on to care for someone else, either. Maybe things will change in the future; no one can tell. Things may go differently, something may happen—who knows, right?

Naturally, I know *nothing* will change, and moving on is probably the only way; I can't follow it right now, but I may have to try soon. At any rate, I felt I should write you a long text once again, because today I acted weird; I'm in a very bad place right now—for which you are not at fault—and I can't stop thinking of all these things—particularly, that I can't make you be here, when I need you, because it makes you feel awkward. You talked about changes: you've changed during the time I've known you— twice. First, when I met you and we started hanging out; second, when you realized you are not allowed to have feelings for me.

When the feelings die—for both of us—maybe our friendship can flourish, because there won't be any reason for you to think you're doing something wrong by being around me. But, for now, I guess I just have to learn to live with what I can get, and not ask for more—mostly, because I do not desire to ask you for more than you are willing to offer. I guess, seeing you today was more than enough.

I'm sure I'm wrong in some things, so feel free to correct me, if you want; I'm even more certain I'm wrong in sending you this, but I guess I felt, once again, the need to explain myself—and, most importantly, to let you know how awful I feel for some things, mainly because I know I'm to blame for some of your problems, or at least for some of the thoughts that might have, once, tormented your mind, and because you're not to blame at all for how I feel.

26/11/2014
(written while drunk; sent high on crack)

I'm sorry. Is there a worse phrase in any language? Do we even mean it, when we apologize? What is it that drives us to apologize for what we do, for how we feel? Is *love* something we should be sorry for? Is proclaiming this very love, is saying what hurts us, something worth apologizing for?

Sometimes, perhaps it is; not inasmuch as because we feel sorry, but because we understand that our feelings, our actions, our words had a hurtful impact on someone else. That's what an apology is for; we apologize for what our actions caused. We shouldn't regret what we did, mistake or not doesn't matter, as long as it was something we wanted to do, something that felt right at the moment. A kiss, a heartfelt "I love you", a tight, long embrace, even a simple pleading glance. Perhaps, they have a bigger impact on someone than we dare imagine, yet, as long as they're genuine, they are not things we should feel sorry for.

Hence, I cannot possibly find it in myself to apologize for everything I've said, nor for what I've done. How can I say I'm sorry, for saying I love you? It was in my heart, it's how I feel; it simply came out. I know it was hurtful, something you didn't wish to hear, but I couldn't help it. Can I say I'm sorry for other things I've done? Can I say I'm sorry for kissing you, when it's what haunts my dreams? How can I apologize for what I dream, when, at this point in my life, that simple, yet impossible, dream is what makes my life a bit brighter?

I know the dream's dead, I should have understood it way earlier; I know I should stop dreaming, that I should stop loving you, that I should stop hoping one day the dream will come true. I know now that it will never happen—there's no way I'll ever see the dream come true and thus, by keep on dreaming, I simply prolong my own torture. It's not a fault of yours, though, for you were adamant: "There is no hope!" I was just too stubborn, or too caught up in the beauty of the dream, to allow myself to believe you.

Now I do, though. Hope is dead. It hurts, yes; it even hurts to type it. Yet, it's the only truth that matters. Maybe the rest you've said are, or were at the time, true too. Maybe they weren't. Probably you've regretted saying most things; you certainly regret several things that were done. Do not apologize, though, unless the things you said and did were untrue, unfelt, forced.

I will forever cherish the moments, the memories, the image of your smile that has been branded on my brain. Yet, it's time for me to kill the dream—I pull the plug and listen to its final gasp. The dream's dead; the love will soon follow, and thus the pain shall go away. Back to a life of no emotions, a life, where I have nothing to break my heart.

Still, a piece of my heart will forever to you belong, and that will never change. Even if I know your heart fully belongs to someone else, even if I know your mind desires to be with only one person, a piece of my heart—the only part of it that is still capable of feeling love and care—will remain with you, if only to remind you that once upon a time someone fell madly in love with you and was about to give up the life he knew for you. Now, however, it's time to say "fuck it".

I'll never leave you, I'll remain your friend; this will never change. However, I'll stop dreaming, I'll stop thinking that you'll walk through my door with the intention to stay. I know, now I've finally accepted it, that we'll always have to say goodbye; that we'll never say goodnight in person, but only through texts. Your heart and mind and soul desire next to someone else to sleep and I have to learn with it to live. I'm beginning to accept that my love was doomed—I see now the signs I should have seen from the start. I was blinded by foreign emotions and feelings, by an enthusiasm I never before had experienced. It's all I can say. I can't sleep, can't write, can't even read properly. Your image pops up in my mind like a lovely mirage; thoughts of a different life—where you and I are together—torture my mind constantly. Yet, I do not wish to drink to erase the thoughts, because they remain beautiful, even if they are a persistent reminder of what I'll never possess.

You have what you desire, someone who loves you unconditionally, and whom you also love. Perhaps, you really meant that you dreamt of us; you were quick the dream to kill. I am the one delaying the inevitable, perhaps because I have nothing to fall back to. You had a life, a love, before I appeared. As for me, prior to you I had nothing to show, but for a meaningless existence, barely going through the motions.

And still, after experiencing love, after finally learning how it really feels to have your heart broken in two, I can still say "thank you". Thank you, thus, for showing me I had love in me, and thank you for letting me believe, even for a second, that there was a chance for my life to turn around. The chance is gone, the hope is dead and I know I'll soon go back to my previous way of living. Maybe it's for the best, too; eventually, you'll get tired of me, you'll remain faithful to the only one you truly want and love, while I'll live a life, where there is no pain, no tears, no more heartbreak and misery.

I'll go back to a life I know so well, and you'll start feeling better for yourself, because you'll be devoted to the one you want. No excuses, no more empty words. I wish to believe that you meant what you said, yet I find it hard to accept it. Not because it makes my choice easier, but because your choices indicate the truth I find so hard to swallow.

Back to where I belong I slowly go, the road to destruction once again I follow. The end is nigh, I can feel it. A bottle of whisky awaits me, I already smell it. I'll leave it untouched for now, though, for I still wish to remember you; I do not wish to forget what took place, I have no intention of forgetting the best three months of my life. Eventually, though, I'll drink. Eventually, my last promise shall be broken; I can't be around forever, mostly because you won't let me. You have someone else to care for, someone else you love, and to him you have to return and your attention devote.

I was merely a distraction; I appeared at the right time to take your mind away from your problems. You saw an escape in me—you nearly took it. At the last moment, you regretted it. You realized you couldn't do it; there was no way you could abandon him you so much love. Perhaps, you did dream that things were different—allow me to believe that, at least for a short while, I occupied your dreams.

Now, I do not belong there anymore; perhaps righteously so. You'll always haunt my dreams, you'll always be the reminder of a life I could have had. That life is dead, though, and so are my dreams and hopes. No more shall I dare believe things could be different—there was never a hope to begin with. We created it, because we needed it. Once you realized it was a mistake, you hurriedly killed it. I was more stubborn, I let it be on life support for a while, because I didn't have the balls to say goodbye to my most beautiful dream.

Farewell I say to the dream and six feet under I bury its ashes. Sometimes, loving someone means letting them go—that's exactly what I am doing. I am letting you go, because I love you. I can't be the reason for your tears, I can't be the reason for your struggle. You're free, return to what you know as safe, familiar; return to the one you love. Only remember, I loved you immensely, and still do. Even when you feel down, remember that, no matter what, I shall forever love you.

I'm afraid it won't fade away; therefore, I'm leaving—thus, breaking the last remaining promise. Not because I don't wish to be around you—it pains me more than you can imagine even typing these words— but precisely because I can't stop wishing to be with you. It will never happen, you made it perfectly clear, and therefore I'm leaving, to let you live the life you truly desire, with the one you wish to be by your side till death do you part. As for me, I go back to my other mistresses, the alcohol, the cigarettes, the one-night stands. Back to a life of abuse, where I will find my writing spirit; you shall forever be my true muse, but I have to let you go.

Therefore, there is no apology; I hurt you, but I didn't mean to. I love you, and will never stop. I'm leaving, because I must. For the first, and last, time in my life, I'm doing what's *right*, what I *ought* to do, and it hurts more than I had dared imagine. And so the "nice guy" is dead; the final time I do what's right. I put a bullet in his head and he's gone—"No More Mr. Nice Guy" Alice Cooper sang and I finally understand the meaning of the song.

> *Dark clouds of sorrow above my head hover,*
> *Rain pours down, acidic water my skin burns.*
> *I don't run, I don't hide, I simply take it.*
> *Nothing to the pain in my heart can compare,*
> *Yet I remain, wishing for a new wound.*
> *Something the pain to take away,*

A medicine for a broken heart.
I hear the roar of the wild storm,
I see the waves come crushing down.
On the rock I stand, wishing away to be taken,
To the bottom of the ocean to be driven.
With the fish and wrecks to lie, for eternity.
A harbor of no purpose, a ship with no destination.
A wingless bird, a legless predator.
A snake without a mouth,
A tree without roots nor branches.
I lay alone, the dark engulfs me,
And I wish within it to remain.
I see the sun and I cry;
A new day begins,
The end hasn't come.
Why? I cry. No one listens.
A new day, the same pain.
Unchanging days, a circle of pain and of tears.
Why? I cry again, still no reply.
You're away, and I'm still here.
Why? For the last time I cry and close my eyes.

08/12/2014
(written and sent after chugging down a bottle of
cheap red wine and while sipping on the second)

My dearest S.,

First, let me apologize for what I'm about to say; believe me, it's not easy to write these things, let alone knowing that you'll read them. How will they affect you, I ask myself. I don't like the answer, I must admit, but, I'm afraid it's the only way, the only feasible solution. For three months has this situation being ongoing, and I'm afraid a certain point has been reached; the dreadful point of pointlessness. And, I'm not apologizing beforehand because I regret saying these things; I do feel bad, when I think of how my words may affect you, but, I do not regret sitting down and typing them: in as much as I never felt sorry for telling you "I fucking love you", I do not regret what comes next.

So, to begin with, I honestly believe we're just kidding ourselves by continuing our ongoing text-discussions, by seeing each other, and, most importantly, by telling ourselves that we'll be able to be just friends. We'll never be *just* friends; personally, I do not believe anyone can be friends with someone they fell in love with. It's something that will forever hover over our heads, even if we do get over those feelings. I'm quite sure you've actually gotten over most feelings, because it's the "right" thing to do, and hence you were quick to kill whatever dreams you may have had about us, but I haven't, obviously. I still live in that dreamworld of mine, where you one day may be mine—I still keep the hope alive that one day you won't have to go home, but *home* will be staying with me. Stupid dreams, I know, and hopeless thoughts, but, as it turns out, I'm way more romantic than I've ever wanted to even believe.

Nevertheless, I'm finally beginning to see the harsh reality; I haven't stopped dreaming, but, nowadays, there's nothing beautiful about those dreams. Don't get me wrong, the dreams, on their own, are still wonderful, but, the feelings they evoke in me aren't. Dreaming of you, of us being together, of us sitting on my couch reading, or just talking, dreaming of kissing you without having to feel guilt afterwards, dreaming of spending the rest of my life with you, hurt more than I can possibly describe—

dreaming of all these things make me wish to remain in bed until I breathe my last breath, for the dreams are a grave reminder of the morbid reality; they're there to remind me that they'll forever remain dreams. And, I think I've mentioned it once, I do not like living in dreams—I prefer dreaming about things that I can actively pursue, that I can, given the right circumstances, actually achieve. And, naturally, I cannot do that with this specific dream—I could, of course, actively pursue you, but, I realize it would get me nothing, it would lead me nowhere. Moreover, I do not wish to complicate things even more for you. Despite everything, I do still care more about your happiness than mine.

And that brings up the point of "mocking each other". I have, indeed, changed for your sake, I did commit to those changes, because I wanted to make you happy—probably, also because I wished to show you I'm willing both to commit to something and to actively change. I would have never quitted drinking for as long as I did, if it wasn't for you, if it wasn't for knowing that I would disappoint you, and sadden you, if I started drinking again. Yet, can I really change? Can I really commit? Unfortunately, I believe I can, but, as I see my dreams fading away—suffering a slow, painful death—faster and faster, I also realize I cannot keep these changes only with the vain hope of something impossible. Hence, I'm "mocking" you, in the sense that, without something worth the waiting and the committing, I cannot retain the changes. We'll never be together, thus I'll eventually start drinking again, I'll revert back to my old life—and that's something you don't need to see. As for your "mocking", I honestly believe that, especially lately, you're just keeping me as a life vest, just in case the boat, that is your relationship, suddenly hits an iceberg and sinks. I was never your "harbor"; your "harbor" should have been your boyfriend, after all, since that's the purpose of a relationship, to have someone to return to, no matter how bad things are. Yet, you called *me* your "harbor", and who knows, maybe you even meant it, for a while. Yet, I doubt you believe it now, nor can I accept that you believe, or ever believed, other things you told me. Did you fall in love with me, as you once said? Maybe. I highly doubt it, though. It's nice to try and believe it, but a voice in my head tells me I shouldn't, that it was a lie. I'm afraid a lot of things you told me are lies; impressively enough, even if you refuse to believe it, I haven't lied to you. Maybe that's another thing that hurts; that, for once in my life, I was the honest part of a human relationship. Regardless of whether you were honest or not with me, the matter of the fact is, you let me have the hope, you created the dreams. It wasn't your fault that I fell for you—I blame my stupid brain for that—but, it was your fault for not pushing me away, when that happened. It was your fault for feeling the same way, it was your fault for staying around, obviously because you liked the situation, but, perhaps, also because you thought, albeit only partly, that it might be nice, if some of the dreams came true. I doubt it, though, you still wish for those dreams to come alive; whatever it was that you were thinking in the beginning, has now finally died within you. You wish to stay with your boyfriend, you wish to erase whatever you felt for me, you wish to continue the life you think righteous and perfect; feel free to do so, but do not expect that I can stick around and see you enjoy life with your boyfriend—you'd hate it, after all, if I found someone else.

I once told you that "goodbye is the only way"; ironically, when I said that, I didn't realize at the time that I was talking to myself, that I was referring to *us*; and yes, that's the only conclusion that can be drawn from this letter, but also from the past three months. Goodbye is, indeed, the *only* way. I do not wish to lose you, it hurts me more than you can imagine even typing these words, let alone thinking I'll give them to you to read them, *but*, it is the only way we have. To continue doing what we've been doing for the past months would be utterly idiotic. You are *never* going to leave your boyfriend, for various reasons, and I am not capable of simply erasing my love for you and become your friend. You coming back to my place ignites the flame of the dreams; you leaving my place, to go back to him, makes me want to die. I can't have that any longer. I would welcome you with open arms, if I knew there was hope for us to get together. Were you to break up, and just made me wait for a long while, in order to ensure I can change for good, I would be willing—Hell, I'd be glad—to commit to the changes. What's the difference, you ask? If I knew that hope was still alive, I wouldn't have to write these lines, my heart wouldn't ache this much. "No hope" and I finally see the truthfulness in those two hurtful words.

There's nothing left to be said, but a huge thank you for showing me that I am capable of loving, of changing, of committing. I do not regret meeting you, I do not regret spending three months around you, nor do I regret letting myself fall in love with you. I only wish that things were different, that I had met you in a different time, where my dreams might have had a shot of coming true. I didn't, that's life, and I need to accept it and move on. So do you; you have to forget that you let yourself fall for someone third, and focus on maintaining your relationship, since it's what you truly desire. So, thank you for the good moments, the memories, and for having been in my life.

I will forever keep you in my heart,
G.

15/12/2014
(written and sent in a sober condition)

My dearest S.,

Let me start by saying, I'm sorry. For what, it's for me to know.

So, going against all rules about good writing, I'll begin from the ending. This is the final goodbye.

Since I've spoiled the ending, maybe you won't even read the rest of these lines, so, perhaps, I'm just wasting my time even typing them—on the other hand, maybe you'll decide to read them anyhow, even if you know the ending.

The story begins in a small briefing room, circa 5 months ago; I walked in, ready to abandon Denmark and my studies, go back to Greece and enter the pointless game of struggling to get a job, moving back to my parents and, in general, I was ready to abandon life as a whole. Then, I happened to see a sweet-looking girl; I sat next to her, she smiled at me. It felt nice, it made me smile inwardly. Afterwards, that same girl started talking to me—in fact, she started the conversation just a few seconds before I did.

After that, we started talking often; we spent an entire weekend chatting over Facebook; we went out that next Monday—only a week after we first met—and it was the most fun date I've ever had. She did mention, albeit briefly, that she's in a serious relationship, but she said it in a way that contained an underlying message that the relationship was near its end. After the date, we continued chatting, through both Facebook and text messages. We met often, we went out for coffee and tea, we had long discussions and, in general, I had the greatest time—my dates with that girl were some of the highlights of my life.

Then, about two or three weeks after I met her, she asked me to use my couch for the night. Naturally, I said yes, for I had promised her that my couch was available. I still wonder why she came to me. Nonetheless, she came, in a vulnerable state, but, because I really liked her, I spent the night comforting her. Just sitting with her on the couch, holding her tight to comfort her, felt better than anything else that might have happened.

The next morning, she left early, for she had reconciled with her boyfriend. However, she left her toothbrush behind. At first, I got excited, I thought she was thinking of returning. I talked to my friends over Skype the following days; they were all impressed with my excitement, the beautiful words I used to describe both the girl and the night she slept on my couch. Moreover, they were slightly worried about me, because I was willing to drastically change my life for that girl's sake. I had no problem letting her stay in my apartment for a while, if she indeed broke up, and, if she did end up with me, I was willing to change, at least on paper, my religion, if it would make her life easier. They thought I was nuts, yet, I was adamant. I was willing to sacrifice my way of living, if it meant I'd have that girl in my life forever.

We had our first fight, when she thought I gave her an ultimatum, in regards to choose between her boyfriend and I. She said that "it is beautiful to dream", in terms of our being together, but she also said she "would hate myself, if she didn't try to save her relationship" and that "she can't choose between two people". I respected that, even if it was the first stab in the heart I received from that girl. However, the stab was subtle and I ignored it—yes, I was that naïve and stupid.

The days turned to weeks, and she never came back, to stay. I began believing she simply forgot her toothbrush, that I was interpreting things the way I wanted to. Then, one day, she came to me, a day after she had told me she had a huge fight with her boyfriend. She told me they had reconciled, then, we ended up kissing—I forgot to mention, I had promised her that I wouldn't kiss her, unless it meant we'd be together, because I truly wanted her to be my "last first kiss". Nonetheless, she made me break that promise and we kissed. She also said "no hope" after we kissed—she meant, we'd never be together. I refused to believe her, at first, because I thought I saw hope in her eyes, but mostly, because I was blinded by love.

After that, it took her a couple of weeks, before she returned to my apartment, just for a visit. Those were some of the most dreadful weeks of my entire life; I couldn't sleep, I felt like shit, I didn't want to do anything. She kept on talking to me through texts, and we did go out, *but*, she wouldn't return to my apartment, and it was killing me slowly.

Eventually, she returned. We went back into being "just friends", sort of, at least. We had a nice time together, even if we often ended up talking about us, which was a topic that caused some heartbreak to me, and possibly to her too.

At some point, she decided she shouldn't tell

me a few things, in particular what was happening at home, with her boyfriend. I respected it, even though, deep down, I wanted to know. She claimed, however, that it was "so that she won't put more wood into the fire". One day, then, when she was at my place, she said "I love you", and that "I kissed him (in reference to her boyfriend) and dreamt of you, I slept with him, and dreamt of you". I also told her, "I fucking love you"; it was the first time in my life I uttered the L-word, and also the first time that I actually was in love with someone. That night, we kissed again, the final time we kissed—up to this point, I still cherish the memory of our awkward kisses.

We maintained a good relationship since that second, and last, kiss, although things were definitely changed; the girl had, once again, cheated on her boyfriend, whom she still loved, or so, at the very least, she claimed, and that undoubtedly made her feel awkward and weird. On the other hand, that didn't stop her from coming back to my place a few times; we watched movies, we talked, we laughed. Of course, we had to stop talking about us, since the subject would always worsen things, would make things feel weirder.

Once, during the end of this "relationship/ friendship/whatever-the-fuck-it-may-be-called", she abruptly came to my place, after a meeting with a professor that didn't end well. She laid down on my couch, trying to sleep, while she sobbed; I just sat on the couch reading. It was one of those moments that still haunt my dreams, because, even if only for a short while, I actually saw my dream come alive. It felt as if we were, indeed, living together—which had been my most beautiful dream for almost as long as I knew her.

Perhaps, though, after that, she saw something changing; maybe, the fact she sought comfort and refuge to me, instead of her boyfriend, told her something about her relationship, about how good or bad things really were at the time. Or, maybe, she just questioned herself on whether she was doing the right thing, because her "harbor" wasn't her boyfriend, but someone she knew for 4 or so months.

Nevertheless, the last few weeks of our acquaintance (as good a term as any), were slightly weird. I began realizing that we should say goodbye. I started comprehending that her relationship was actually good; she kept on texting me almost constantly—which was a way for both of us to compensate for the lack of each other's physical presence. She even texted me during her anniversary with her boyfriend and on her birthday; days, where she supposedly had to spend with the man she wished to marry and grow old with.

And, then came the final day. The day she came to my apartment again, one day before I was to go back to Greece for the Christmas holidays. At first, things went well, we talked about general stuff and we laughed. Then, she asked me "are you okay?"; a question, which at first I didn't want to answer. Finally, though, I succumbed to my aching heart and spoke.

I told her my thoughts, how I believed that "goodbye was the only way". She once again reaffirmed the "no hope". A final stab through my heart and it was finally torn into a thousand pieces. However, my love for her managed to overcome everything else, and, when she decided she wanted to go back home, to run away from me and whatever might have happened, she told me, as a goodbye, that things were going great with her and her boyfriend, that she had already chosen him, instead of me.

She had made her decision, and yet, she

persisted on being around me, on seeing me and talking to me non-stop. Fortunately, I was in such a vulnerable state, due to my heartache, that I actually talked sweet to her, promised her that I didn't want to lose her. And, quite frankly, I believed it. I didn't want to let her go, and I hate the fact I lost her.

On the other hand, I also feel immense relief that she's no longer in my life. I finally feel free. I exploded after she left my place, I destroyed my closet, I torn the postcard she had once sent me into pieces—I see the poesy in it, since she had torn my heart into tiny pieces—I cried like a little baby and then I finally felt my mind clearing up. The fog had been lifted and I was my old self. I felt liberated for knowing she won't be in my life anymore. I spent 4 months of my life hoping for a dream that was stillborn. I wasted my time for a hope that never had existed.

I can't forget the good times and I sincerely wish that things were different. I still dream of her sleeping next to me, of waking up for the rest of my life and seeing her. Yet, it's never going to come true, and I'm okay with it. In fact, if there's anything I regret, is that I didn't have the chance to tell her a proper goodbye, when she ran, for the last time, away from me, to hide into her boyfriend's embrace.

And that's the story I wanted to tell you, and so, there's nothing left to say, *but* a GOODBYE.

26/01/2015
(written and sent during a 3-day drinking binge)

Peaceful nights on the couch, watching movies and reading books; cooking dinner and eating together every afternoon; holding each other throughout the night; having long—and often heated—discussions on various general matters; seeing you smile at every occasion; gazing into your eyes and getting lost in your glance; long walks, where I'd nag, although, deep down, I'd enjoy the fact you make sure I remain healthy; knowing I have a reason to live for, namely to make sure you're happy for the rest of your life.

Long fights, because of the peculiarities of my character; a struggle to stay away from the drinks and the rest of my bad habits; mutual irritation towards each other's differences; nights where we'd both wish we weren't together; regrets for leaving other things behind; dreams of a different life.

That's how I've imagined—and, I must hereby admit, from a very early point in our acquaintance— our life might have developed, had we been together. It was, however, beautiful to dream, not only because of the good parts, but also for the bad ones. Precisely because I know, or at least I felt—and still dare do— that in good and bad, we'd always find a way to resolve the issues; speaking from my side—which is, after all, the only side I can talk of—I know I'd do anything to ensure that, regardless of differences, fights, etc., I'd always make up for my stupid acts and would try to keep you happy until the inevitable end of death.

Unfortunately, I didn't pay much attention at the time to the fact that you already had someone in your life doing those very things, and for whom you also did the same things. You made Denmark feel home, you made me think I'd be glad to come back, because you'd be here, waiting for me. Again, I completely ignored the fact Denmark was already home for you; you already had, and still have, someone waiting for you here, you have a person to come back to here in Denmark, aside from all the other reasons you have. For me, you were the only reason, and now that it has been taken away from me, I find myself back into a familiar position: not having a clue of what I want in my life, wishing to go away, to start anew (once again), to go back home to what's familiar to me, or to a new place, where I'll start from zero, with no memories, no past, no regrets, no pain.

You gave me the freedom of choice, in regards to us; I'm the one to decide. In all honesty—and sometimes I can be brutally honest—I guess I cannot make that choice. It's all too complicated in my mind, namely because I know what I ought to do, what I want to do, and what I'm going to do. What I ought to do, is to let you go, to start anew; you gave me great memories, you made me fall in love, you made me dream and desire a life, which I had never previously considered. What I want to do, is be around you, preferably all the time; I still want to hug you tight and long, I still want to kiss you, I still want to see my dreams come true. What I am going to do is a combination of the two, for the simple, sole reason that I cannot do otherwise. I see no feasible way of driving you away, but, at the very same time, I also know that there is no hope for my dream to come true. Definitely, things aren't going to be the same with us, but, I'm not trying to push you away—I can't let you go, obviously. Yet, I'm trying to be colder than before, mainly in order to avoid acting upon my deepest desires and kiss you, thus re-entering into the endless circle we've already been through. That's also the reason you haven't gotten your box of tea back yet; it symbolizes a hope that you'll come back to my place, eventually. It also symbolizes that you'll always leave, while it remains. I cannot part with it, because I still want to believe in the ghost of hope of you one day coming, without the need to leave.

I may owe you an explanation on one thing of late, namely, why I'm often in a bad mood, every time we're together. It's because I'm in a constant conflict with myself, with my ought to do and want to do. When I step out of the door, knowing I'm to meet you and spend time with you, everything else goes blank within me. I tell myself it's time to end this, to put an end to my misery—and, subsequently, stop making you sad, because of my awful mood—but, the moment I lay eyes on you, the second I see you smile and you gaze into my eyes, I realize it's impossible for me to let you go, to lose you from my life.

You may have noticed it already, but I don't have a lot of people I hold dear. This Christmas, I let loose another friend; we didn't have a fight, but, it became mutual understanding that the disagreements in our characters are too much for us to remain friends. I hold you dear—I hope you know that, even if I don't always show it—and losing you will cost me a lot; I've lost a lot of friends, acquaintances, etc., throughout my life, yet, I can't let you go, despite knowing you for only five months. The main issue, though, is that, even though I care for you as a friend too, we can never be *just* friends; the reasons for that, I think you know them already. I wish that you are happy, and remain thus, within your relationship, but, I'm not strong enough to stay around to see that happening. Nor am I in any stand whatsoever to forget my dreams, or erase my emotions towards you. Yes, there have been times, where I tried to erase my feelings, my memories of you, times where I tried to hate you, to make letting you go easier. It didn't work, it can't work.

Whether it's an excuse or a cruel reality, I cannot with certainty say, but, perhaps, it's my need to write, the voice in my head that guides my writing, that is guiding me into these impossible predicaments. Perhaps, I willingly devoted myself into the impossible dream of one day waking up next to you, because I saw a way towards heartbreak and devastation. Perhaps, thus, it's all my fault, because by being miserable, depressed, plagued by a strong desire to drink and by suicidal thoughts, I can write better; I've tried writing, while happy, and it didn't go that well. Potentially, that's also the reason I remain in Denmark; being here makes me miserable, and maybe that guides my writing too. Maybe I am paying for my art, maybe, like so many before me, I have to go through Hell several times, for the sake of my craft. On the other hand, maybe I'm just delusional in regards to my talent and I'm just a moron, who lives in an imaginary world. I don't know. But, in the end, perhaps it's for the best that we're in the current situation; who's to say that, if we had somehow ended up together, I wouldn't, subconsciously even, sabotage the whole thing, if it made me too happy, just to recapture my writing? A voice in my head insists that I would gladly sacrifice the writing, if it meant being happy with you, but, maybe, the voice is wrong, or misleading. Or, maybe, it speaks the truth. I don't know which of the two possibilities hurts the most.

At least, this text has a purpose of showing you, somewhat, what's going on in my head. Definitely it's mostly centered around you, for obvious reasons, although I cannot say you're the sole reason of my suffering. Most possibly—and I do mean that I don't know for certain—you're not even the main reason for the Hell I'm going through. However, I did see a way out of Hell in you; what happened next, and how that went, I think you already know, or at least have a good idea thereof. Maybe, that's why I'm, at least recently, so cold and mean towards you; because I saw a way out, and then it was taken away. I don't begrudge you, though; it's not your fault that I willingly ignored all the signs about how I should have never let myself dream the things I dreamt. I don't want you to apologize for anything; you've done that already, even though I have never blamed you. Besides, an apology, for better or for worse, is not capable of mending the wounds.

What do I try to accomplish with this? I don't know. Maybe, it will make you go away from me; maybe, it'll scare you and drive you away, because you'll see in me a threat to your domestic peace, to the status quo you've known for so long. Definitely—I'm not delusional—I have no doubt that I won't ever hear a knock on the door, only to see you standing on the other side—that's something that has been reserved for my dreams. If I've learned anything all these years, is that dreams do not come true; our lives are novels, but they do not have happy endings.

18/02/2015
(written after a junk injection; sent while sober)

It's been a Hell since we last said goodbye; it was for the final, last time, yet, I wouldn't be able to hold it, I knew it from the moment we hugged for what it felt like the last time. And how could I stay away?

Yes, we should stay away from each other; yes, the goodbye ought to be ultimately final; yes, we must never see each other again. All the "shoulds" and "oughts" and "musts"; all the notions of what's "right" and what's "wrong". Even if I comprehend them, down to their core, I cannot accept them, nor am I willing to embrace them.

When it doesn't feel "right" down to the core of

my own soul and mind, how can I accept something as fundamentally "right"? Moreover, what *is* fundamentally "right"? Has anyone at any point in history described with certainty, without fallacies and hesitation, what can be considered fundamentally "right"? No!

We have all the religion textbooks and all philosophical works telling us what to believe in, what to think as "right" and what to think as "wrong". But, are these writers in stand to tell us, without a shadow of a doubt, that action x is "right", or that action y is "wrong"? Definitely not. Simply because they created their own notion of "right" and "wrong" upon convictions of a false God, or gods. They created a philosophy, claiming to know what's "right" and what's "wrong" for their own personal reasons; maybe, they wanted to convey a general message, maybe they had grand political aspirations, maybe something else; who gives a fuck. The fact of the matter is we don't know what is fundamentally "right" and "wrong", we just live by some false convictions someone sometime managed to convey to us, through some outdated text, we still consider a sacred relic, and damned be those that deny it!

I don't claim to know "right" from "wrong"; on the other hand, I can honestly say how I feel, after we separated, because it was the "right" thing to do: I felt like shit, I've gone through ten stages of Hell, and I still feel like shit. I'm trapped in the vilest pit of Hell, suffering in the grip of Dante's three-headed Devil, munched by the horrid heads, alongside history's greatest sinners. I suffer daily, every single minute, because I cannot see you, because I cannot hold you.

Yes, I understand why we had to say farewell for good, and why you'd never try to reach out for me again. You have someone else, you have a life that must needs be preserved, someone you must keep happy till the end of days, and I'm only a sad reminder of a different possibility, of a different choice; you wish I stayed away, for, while I'm around, I'm a temptation you cannot deny—all holy men managed to deny Devil's temptations, and thus you also wish to do, but you're not as strong as those holy men— either madmen, who heard voices, or hypocrites that convinced us all they could communicate with an entity that never existed.

I also have a life of my own and demons to confront; and, perhaps, my kind of Hell is way worse than yours. For you, it's all about keeping a promise you gave to someone way before you met me—I came along, I perhaps made you question that promise, but, at any rate, you were adamant in keeping it, for which I actually admire you. However, the fact of the matter is while I worsened things for you, while I perhaps created a Hell, where there was none, *you* made me escape my own personal Hell.

Let me, thus, elaborate: since we said the final goodbye, I've returned back to my own Hell. While you were around, while there was still some vague hope—and even when you outright murdered it, but remained in my life—I could escape Hell, I could live a "normal" life, the one that most people enjoy without even realizing it. You left my life, for good, I returned the tea box and I gave up all chances of ever seeing you again; thus, I walked straight back to Hell. All voices, demons, monsters in my head were awakened, and they were happy for it, for they were tired of the waiting.

How could I refuse them, though? Since you were gone, forever, how could I find the testicular fortitude to deny their advances, their demands, their needs? I let them take over, and it felt fine; yes, of course, I returned to a state of depression, I willingly went back to a state, where death seemed the best out of all options available. On the other hand, I could once again write, I could create, and, despite the constant wishing for death, I was able to live. Contradictory as it may sound, it's how it feels; death is salvation, but writing is the escape from the misery of living. I went back to the drinking and the smoking; I tried to go back to the fucking, as well, but I'm not ready yet— I'm still too attached to you, to be able to properly pursue new faces in my life. I'm still clinging hard onto the memory of you sleeping next to me, to be mentally able to replace that memory with someone new. Nevertheless, that shall come too, and then, it'll all be over.

You were the bright light in a tunnel dark; you were the first ever to hear about the monsters in my head, about the Hell that exists within my own soul. You were the first, and in many a-cases the only, to hear about the thoughts of death, the insanity of everyday life, the pointlessness of my existence. And you stood by me, despite all that; you didn't run away, you remained, and tried, albeit in vain, to help me. For that, I shall forever be grateful to you.

Moreover, you ignited something within me, a new flame of creativity, which sparked new horizons for the only thing I know how to do, for the only thing I was born to do; without you, my writing would have remained stale, boring, uninspiring. You showed me the real way, and opened up new horizons, new lands to explore, new ways to fight the demons and the monsters. They will never be defeated, but, at least, you provided me with means to keep on fighting them for a while longer. Additionally, your presence in my life gave me strength and courage to continue fighting them; I will never win the war, but I did win some battles—if it wasn't for you, those battles would have been lost, and perhaps, now, instead of writing you this, I would be six feet under, the losing side of a fierce war. Unfortunately, I can't say with conviction whether it's a good thing I actually won those battles.

Whatever the case, we've gone our separate ways; we both returned to the lives we were familiar with. And it's alright; at least, I know you have a chance of finding true happiness, of enjoying life in accordance to what you believe in, and what you wish for the future. And that's what matters to me; to know you're happy, to know you're having a reason to smile every single morning. It pains me more than anyone could possibly imagine to know it's because of someone else you're smiling, but, as long as you are, indeed, smiling genuinely, I will bear the pain.

As for me, I'm sorry, but I cannot be okay, I cannot be alright, and I can definitely not be happy; I wasn't meant to be any of those aforementioned things. My wiring is such, that I will go unhappy for the rest of my pathetic existence. Hopefully, I'll be able to produce some memorable works before I leave this world forever, so my birth won't go completely to waste, but, other than that, I cannot be happy; I was born a sad, miserable bastard, and thus shall I also die. On the other hand, I think it's important for you to know that you did make me happy; whenever I held you in my arms, I was happy. Whenever you looked into my eyes, and I could read "love" in your glance, I was happy. Every single time I was around you, I was happy. The night you slept in my arms, the one single night I could hold you, and kiss you, until we both fell asleep, I felt like I actually deserved a "normal" life.

My heart would skip a beat every time I saw you, every time I hugged you. Despite of how I felt, when the time to say goodbye came, regardless of the countless stabs that have gone through my heart whenever you had to go home, I was still smiling, when you sent me a text; I would still feel joy, when we continued to talk through texts—even if, deep down, I knew you were home, with someone else. I was able to bypass all that, because you showed me what happiness meant.

Now, it's all gone; and it's alright, because, by showing me happiness, you deprived it of yourself. I was the "wrong", I was the egregious mistake. You wished something else, you desired someone else, and, when all is said and done, it's alright, too. Not because I can accept it and move on, but because I hope it's what you truly desire. As long as you smile every single morning, I'm alright. Dead or alive, I'm happy for you; and, if I ever see a tear run from your eye, I shall forever be around, to wipe it away; whether it'll be my body or just my spirit, only time will tell. However, even if I'm dead tomorrow, you should know that my spirit shall linger on, only to ensure that you are happy. Despite of all the broken promises, I can promise you one thing, with certainty, and with no doubts whatsoever:

No matter what happened, or what may happen in the future, I shall always be the person that loved you more than life itself; the one person to whom you meant more than anything, and anyone, else; the one person that considered of giving up everything; and, for all the above mentioned reasons, I shall always be your guardian angel, constantly being around, even if unnoticed, to ensure you're always happy and cheerful, and to wipe away any tears that may run down your beautiful eyes. Regardless of where I am, somewhere in this world, or lost in a different realm altogether, a part of me will always be close to you, making sure you never shed a tear, and to kill any negative emotions before they have the chance to reach your heart.

18/03/2015
(written while drunk; unsent)

Have I missed you, too? Yes. It's a simple answer, requiring nothing but the simplest of all words. However...

I may have missed the good times, when you would open the door to my apartment and come in, when I'd hug you and hold you in my arms, when I'd just talk to you, the night you slept in my bed, the moments we've kissed, the wonderful moments when we stared each other in the eyes, silently, letting our glances do all the talking. Yes, I've missed all the good moments.

I haven't missed the vanity of it all; I do not miss the heartache, the sitting in the dark, dreaming of you and of the things that would never be. The long hours of knowing you're with someone else, the dreams of you and me, that would never be, the knowledge of my dream being dead and the pain it caused; these are the things I haven't missed.

I loved you, that much is true, no matter how much you don't like hearing the L-word. Yet, there's another L-word I sometimes feel about you. It's called "loathing". You changed me, your presence in my life, and everything that transpired, altered my inner being, my mindset, me. And I don't like those changes, especially when I know they were all for nothing. I changed, I lost myself, and for what?

Definitely not in order to spend the rest of

my life with the one person I could easily see waking up next to for the rest of my presence in this world. I changed for a non-existent dream; I came to hate myself for ever falling for you.

Ever since we saw each other last—the two times in the class notwithstanding—I've returned to the writing and the drink; however, I do not drink every day, nor in the same extent as once upon a time. I do not know why, somehow I feel I shouldn't; and I despise myself for it, because the changes I've undergone, for your sake, are still here, reminding me of all the things we've been through, good and bad alike. And I don't like it one single fucking bit.

Would I avoid your mail? I thought about it, yes. I've even thought I should send you this mail, instead of whatever kind of bullshit I'll later fabricate and actually send you. Perhaps, you should know how awful it feels hearing back from you; how terrible it makes me feel knowing that a part of me is willing to let you re-enter my life and once again haunt my thoughts and dreams. By saying goodbye to you, I had the chance to kill a nightmare and escape pointlessness. Few words from you, and here I am, once more ready to throw myself at the lions, voluntarily allowing them to devour the last shreds of my soul.

I am stupid, I know that much. Yet, I'm tired, too. I'm tired of missing you, of thinking about you, of dreaming of you. I was on the verge of leaving Denmark—I'm still trying to figure out what exactly made me doubt that decision. I'm still here, for better or for worse, and that means, there's always another chance of seeing you, of going through the same Hell. I do not want it, I do not desire it. Meanwhile, I still think of holding you, of kissing you, one more time.

It's not going to happen, therefore, why not

maintain the silence, the promise? I promised never to talk to you again, why should I break it? I should ignore the mail, avoid you like the Devil; live and let live. We went our separate ways, why should you ask how I'm doing? Why should you care? If you still miss me, you should reevaluate certain things... but that's not my place, nor do I have any right to talk about it. It's your life, your decisions, your regrets.

Consequently, you must understand one thing: if you feel like you want me back in your life, if you miss me, and all the rest of the horseshit you wrote, it cannot be under the old circumstances. It needs change, it has to be different, otherwise, there's no point in going back into the shithole we had dug ourselves into around Christmas time. If it's the same old, there's no reason to go back into it. "Same old song and dance". I'm sorry, I'm not up for that particular dance.

10/04/2015
(written and sent in the beginning of a long drinking bender)

Yet another mess; no need to apologize, for this mess. I should have seen it coming—I was heading for another heartbreak, but I stayed, and I let the hope be resurrected; I don't know why.

I'm sorry to break the silence pact, I understand that you need time to think, to evaluate, to put things into perspectives, to decide. I only hope you can understand that I also need to know, to have an answer for what is happening, of the whole situation.

I tried to give you all the time you needed, I waited patiently, I... I can't take it anymore. It's been long enough, my mind has been tormented with thoughts, dead dreams, and murdered hopes and I can no longer take it. I don't mean to put pressure on you, nor do I request a full answer, if you're not ready yet to give it. Alas! what I want to know is the generalities; even a general answer of what is going on, without any details, would suffice. What I need, at the moment, is to know where I'm heading to.

I completely understand the conflicts of emotions that must be going on in your head. I haven't been there, but I can imagine how bad it is. If it's bad for me, then it must be Hell for you.

Considering I know nothing of what is going on in your life, nor of what happened, I can only speak for myself; how your first mail, after our "goodbye", made me feel. It made me happy, because you contacted me; it filled me with joy, because you said you missed me, and it was good knowing that you'd missed me, inasmuch as I'd missed you. When you dropped by, after the mail, my heart skipped a beat, it felt great seeing you again. It felt right to walk with you again, to talk to you again. It felt great, when we sat on the couch, and we kissed.

Just as much, it felt great, when you came back, when you visited me after your trip to Germany. The walk on the beach was also exquisite, it warmed me inside to be around you, to talk to you, to just look at you. And, lo! I let myself dream again; I had attempted to kill the dreams, and I had almost succeeded, and yet, when you came back into my life, outright saying things would be different, the dreams were revived in a heartbeat. Consequently, this made me realize one frightening thing: I wasn't over you, no matter how hard I tried to convince both myself and those around me for the contrary. I still had the same feelings for you, I still wished one day we'd end up together. And seeing it come alive, even if only for a while, it made me feel happier than I've ever been.

And then, came the "I still love him, I need to figure out what I want". I almost burst into tears; a dagger went through my heart the moment I read those lines. I saw behind them, a different meaning; inasmuch as you missed me, when we said goodbye, you missed him, when you said goodbye—most probably, you missed him much more than me, because of all the years you've been together. I can't really blame you, it's only natural. I have been around for only a short while, and I'm "the big mistake." Hence, when I received that mail, I saw my newly revived dreams crumble once again into the abyss of nothingness. And, it made me feel worse than all the other times this happened; primarily, because, for once, I actually thought there was a chance for my dream to come true.

I don't know, perhaps, there still is such a chance; I can't know what you're thinking all this time, or whether you're maintaining the silence, because you're back with him and don't know how to tell me. It's all fair; all I want is an answer. As I've said, I need to know, in order to put things in order in my mind.

I can comprehend, if you ultimately wished we'd stay in each other's lives, as good friends; after all, we did share something grand, and you are an inaugural part of my new life. I think, on the other hand, that you already know the reasons why this is not possible. Maybe it's selfish of me not wanting to stay around, in the capacity of a friend, but, it's physically impossible for me. I will always be around, if there's hope for what we both want—although in different levels—to happen and I will be patient, if you need me to be. I don't mind the waiting, as long as there's something awaiting me on the other side. What I won't do is suffer for a dream that's dead.

I see the hypocrisy in talking about being patient, on the one hand, and sending you this, after only a week. I'm sorry, but, I only need one simple answer; if you want, we can keep the silence for longer, as long as you are willing to give me the general outlines, a small summary of what is going on, of where we are standing, of where the situation is heading. I'm not expecting you to have all the answers, I doubt you've had time to figure everything out yet, nor am I requesting it.

I hope to see you, or, at least, to hear from you.

Regardless of everything, I still care about you; as long as you're happy, I can take whatever decision you might have made. The only thing I can't handle, is sitting here, in complete silence, knowing nothing, but how my own heart aches.

20/05/2015
(written and sent during the drinking bender and the constant abuse of junk and blow)

My dear Stella,

Thank you for the silence, for your absence, for your harsh words. You gave me time to think, time to search my soul, and to find all the right answers. I can't stop thinking about you, because you are a main inhabitant of my thoughts and dreams; however, I've been able to take you out of the picture, too, so I could ask myself important, life-altering questions.

The answers are complicated, long, contradicting, terrifying. I've come to realize, I've changed drastically; unfortunately, it's only now I fully comprehend it. It's not you, who brought on the changes—you were merely the trigger that materialized them. Without you, the changes would have remained in the subconscious mind, waiting for a chance to come to life; you barely gave them the opportunity to get a body and become real. Someone else created their very essence; without her, our story would have ended very soon. Sometimes, I do wonder if it would have been better.

Nevertheless, those changes are now real; I do not wish, for my life and future, the same things I would have wished six months ago. I desire different things, a different future than I thought I'd long for. It terrifies me, 'cause it's in unknown waters I find myself swimming, and I have no clue how long I'll last. Regardless, I also find myself determined to remain on the surface, to battle the waves, the sea-monsters, and everything else the dark, deep ocean conceals, and come out victorious. I am not giving up, I cannot give up.

For the first time, I wish to battle the demons and the voices; they had taken control of my life, of my mind, of my very soul, and they were the true inspiration for so long. Finally, I found inspiration outside the realm of Hell, and it felt, mysteriously enough, right. I do not know why, nor how it happened, but, it's one of the conclusions to which I've arrived. Therefore, if I am to keep the new source of inspiration, I must get rid of the old. Change is often horrifying, and thus I tremble in fright, as I write these lines down. Nonetheless, I am willing to give it a real shot, to conquer my fears of the unknown and try to find whatever lies behind the waterfall of fire.

One question, however, remains largely unanswered: what brought on all these changes, what was the spark that made it all happen? I know, for a fact, what the answer is *not*: you. You were, at the most, the final trigger; what blew the breath of life into the changes. Nothing more, nothing less. They were there, ready to come to life, long before you even arrived in my life—perhaps, they would have come to life, regardless of your presence, or absence.

Maybe, the answer's *maturity*, or age. Perhaps, it was bound to happen; I left the teenage boy behind, the one who lived only for the *sex, drugs, and rock n' roll*. Maybe, it was something else; I do not know. And, quite frankly, I do not care enough to search for the ultimate answer. The changes are here, they are legitimate, and they are determined to stay; that's all that matters, in the end. Whatever brought them is insignificant. The bottom line is, they're here to stay.

By thus answering those aforementioned questions, by being tormented day and night by those self-identity questions, I was then, and only then, able to dare bring you back into the picture, curious to see where, and whether, you fit into all this. I allowed myself to remember: with a heavy heart, I brought back all the memories, all the moments, the good and the bad—and there have been plenty of both.

I saw vividly in my mind our first weeks; how we'd go out, talk, have a good time, cheer each other up. Despite the circumstances, regardless of the overall situation, we managed to connect fairly quick, we learned to care for each other, we felt comfortable with each other to talk about things we wouldn't mention to others.

Flashforward to the times of our first collisions; when you said, for the first time, "no hope". When you broke my heart for the first time, out of many. Yet, I remained. Herein lies the first question: why did I remain? What made me stay, despite the clear signs of the pain that was to come? Stubbornness, perhaps. Egoism, maybe. My already growing affection towards you, quite plausibly. I can't say with certainty, but, possibly, it was all three, alongside other feelings. There is no *one* true answer; it was a combination of plenty of thoughts and feelings that made me stay, that forced me to ignore the clear-cut signs of what was approaching fast.

Hence, I stayed. I suffered. I ached, I cried, I despaired. Nonetheless, during both good and bad, your smile was enough to take the pain away, even for a short while. Perhaps, then, I stayed for your smile and for your gaze. The hope of seeing you smile, of seeing your beautiful eyes stare back into mine, was enough to soothe the pain your words and actions caused. Hopefully, I was able to do the same to you; despite the pain and regrets I caused you, I was, too, able to make them all go away, even if only briefly. I'd like to think I did, but I can't know with certainty.

Christmas came; we parted ways rather dramatically. And, for the first time, I was adamant it was all over. Things had reached a certain threshold. We were hurting each other, we were both in pain, because of our relationship. If we were to remain in each other's lives, we'd just kill each other slowly; or so it seemed. I left for Greece with a heavy heart, for we had said the final goodbye in an unfriendly fashion; at the same time, I was glad, too. I felt ready to regain life, to put everything behind and start afresh. The need to talk to you, however, the want to know your whereabouts and how you were doing was too overwhelming. I succumbed, we started talking to each other again. At times, I was angry, I wanted to throw the phone away, while you texted me. At other times, your texts were enough to bring a smile to my face. Once again, I hope your reactions were similar, that some of my texts were able to make you smile, even when you were down.

The return became a reality, we were both back in Denmark. We reconciled, we gave it another shot. It quickly proved to be impossible. For reasons we both know too well. As the final goodbye became evident, as it became a reality we couldn't avoid, our emotions caught on with us. We slept together once, thinking it'd be the last time we'd be around each other. It wasn't enough, it felt too good—for me, at least, and I think for you too, for, otherwise, you wouldn't have remained around. However, it was the beginning of the end. The feelings were too strong and we wanted different things. The final goodbye did arrive; it was harsh, cruel, heart-wrenching. But, it happened, and it felt good. We were both free to pursue what we truly desired, or thought we desired. For a month, or so, I was beginning to recapture everything I had lost—with one difference: the changes you had pushed out of the subconscious and into the conscious remained. I wasn't interested in only the drink and the one-night stand and the writing; I wanted what I had dreamt with you, I was thinking of giving long-term a serious shot.

Then, you re-appeared, as the *ghost of Christmas Past*; you brought back with you all the memories, the smiles, the tears, the hopes and the crushed dreams. I noticed your ring, when I sat next to you in class, and I purposefully was cold towards you; I couldn't go back into the Hell I had just escaped. You came for a second time; I was even colder for I noticed the ring. Then, you contacted me. You told me you came on purpose to class, to see me. You said you'd missed me so fucking much, it hurt.

At first, I felt a warmth overwhelming my heart; I had missed you too, and very much, and it was nice reading you were feeling the same way. And yet, at the same time, I was afraid of letting you back into my life. I thought it'd be the same old song and dance; I was fearful you only wanted me in your life as a "friend"; I thought of ignoring your e-mail, or of sending you a cold "thanks, but no thanks". In the end, I replied positively. I did mention the "same old song and dance", hoping you'd understand.

You surprised me, you visited, unannounced. I felt joy for seeing you again, and some fear; I smelled the heartbreak, the pain that was coming, but I ignored it. We took a walk on the beach, we laughed, we talked. It felt right being around you, but, I was still uncertain of the reasons of your return. When we returned to my apartment, and sat on my couch—which is covered with memories, both sweet and bitter—you kissed me. You said, things would be different and that you can't promise me a "rose garden". Yet, you kissed me again.

You went to Germany; you returned, we saw each other again. We kissed, again, then went to Moesgaard; we spent a long time together, without kissing, but still talking and smiling at each other. Then, you wanted silence. This time, I couldn't hold it. I had to know what was going on; I needed to know, whether you were about to break my heart once again, whether you wanted to return to what you had left behind, whether there was still a chance for us. You told me what had happened, you cried, I held you, we slept together. It felt good; I also knew it was going to be a rocky ride, with its ups and downs, but, I was determined to stay, to embrace the obstacles, and overcome them.

And, for three lovely weeks, things seemed to be going alright; we were taking it slow, no commitment, no grand promises, nothing. We would see each other often, we'd talk often, we'd sometimes share a bed.

We'd cheer each other up; I understand you probably felt more guilt than you showed, when we slept on the same bed, or when we kissed, but, I had no way of knowing it, at the time. You seemed happy, but, maybe, it was all a facade.

Suddenly, you told me you weren't comfortable with us kissing; you had talked to the counselor, had revisited your story, you felt down. I could understand that, and I respected it. Yes, at the time, I was feeling down, and your reaction took me further down. Therefore, I was unable to cheer you up; on the other hand, I do think we had a nice time at *Smageloes* cafe, where we wrote our letters.

I honestly believed that your bad mood would pass, and we'd return in talking, going out, kissing and sleeping together on occasion. I never saw it as commitment, as being in a relationship, nothing of the sort. There were no promises, but that we liked each other's company, and we wanted to do things together. Obviously, I was wrong; I was the only one enjoying those moments. I apologize for misinterpreting the situation, I didn't mean to.

Friday came, I was still in a bad mood; I came to the concert solely because I wanted to see you, because I thought you would be able to cheer me up. I've been wrong before in my life, but never so wildly. I smelled the beer, saw others drinking, the urge awakened and I succumbed. I have a drinking issue, yes. I've also been fighting it for quite some time. Overcoming it isn't easy; it's not something you quit with the snap of the finger, it takes time, patience, understanding. Things went to Hell, I started drinking, and I was focused only on the drink. Hence, Friday went down the way it did.

We met on Tuesday; we talked about serious things and you said how we're not going to be together, how you're not ready to be in a commitment, how you want to enjoy single life. Apparently, *commitment* means different things for each of us: by asking you, if you'd come back to my apartment anytime soon, I didn't in anyway whatsoever think about us committing to anything. Besides, I don't think commitment is an appropriate term; we are individual human beings, we do not need any sort of official bonding, in order to be with each other, to enjoy each other's company. For what is worth, the only reason I didn't think of going out with anyone else during the past few months, is because I didn't want to, not because I felt an imaginary obligation to be only with you. I *want* to be around you, I *want* to hold you in my arms. The fact I am not doing it with anyone else, too, is simply because I do not want to. I just don't have the desire. The word *commitment* implies an obligation to be *only* with one person; personally, I think it's stupid. If both parties truly *want* to be with each other, then, there's no reason to put words into it, to make terms out of it and categorize human relationships. Terms may make speech easier, but that is their only use.

You once asked me, if I would sleep with anyone, when I return to Greece—that was back when you actually wanted, or pretended it was thus, to be in my bed. I said no. The answer's still no. That's because, at the moment, I do not *want* to be with someone else; it may very well change. Same goes for you; if you *want* to be with someone else, there's nothing to hold you. On the other hand, *if* you actually want, even on occasion, to be around me, if you sometimes want us to be like the past few weeks, doing so does not imply a commitment.

Life has no guarantees; there's nothing certain in this life, but death. Therefore, it's important to take full advantage of what life gives us, before it comes to its end. You want to enjoy single life, to go out, rekindle with old friends, flirt with new, exciting people. Do so, by all means. Enjoy it.

You said about taking it slow; I agree, wholeheartedly. We need to learn each other anew, because things are different. I used to dream about you, and, if I am to believe you, you did, too. However, this is a new world order, the circumstances have changed. Hence, we need to start afresh. I guess, all I am asking—and the reason for bringing up the subject this past Tuesday, albeit in my horrible fashion—is that our taking it slow has the prospect of the future in it. As I've noted above, there are no guarantees; I'm not asking for any, nor am I capable of offering any. To put it bluntly: even if we're still in each other's lives ten years down the road, there'll still be no guarantees. If we want to be in each other's lives, we'll have to fight for the right to do so daily. I am willing to do so, I *want* to do so. If you don't, that's alright; we can say the final goodbye, put the last nail in the coffin, and go our separate ways.

If you, on the other hand, do *want* us to be in each other's lives, we'll have to start from zero. We start "dating" again—what that means is, we go out, we talk, we get to know each other all over again. We put, as much as we can, our past behind, we forget everything that transpired between us, and we begin as two strangers. We take things slow, and we let everything develop naturally.

We both have our own issues, we both carry heavy baggage; everyone does. And that's what makes interacting with others exciting. If we were all innocent, pure, perfect, the world would have been a boring place to live in. I'm trying to work on my most serious issues, and you need to work on yours, too. Neither of us is perfect; however, it's those faults of ours that caused the initial physical, and subsequent emotional, attraction between us, which brought us to this, to here.

During the time I've known you, you made me happy, you made me sad, you broke my heart, you made me dream of you, you made me care too much for you, and you made me loathe you. I cannot know how I made you feel, but, I can imagine it has been a similar roller-coaster. That's the main reason we need to start anew, now that the circumstances are different; we have a chance to test whether the dream will be, indeed, beautiful, or if it will turn into a nightmare. The only requirement, commitment if you want, is that we both *want* to be around each other, that we both truly *want* to see whether the "beautiful dream" can come to life. Henceforth, we do not *commit* to anyone, but ourselves, to what we *want*. Naturally, if you do not want, if you prefer to not have me in your life, then, there's no reason to further discuss it; therefore I'm assuming in the last paragraphs, that you actually want me in your life. If you don't, they are meaningless.

Some of the things you've just read, you've heard them before; others, they appear for the first time. Regardless of whether they sound familiar, or not, they're all entirely true. I've used these days of your absence, both physical and text-wise, to focus on a soul-searching journey, through the page. And these are the truthful conclusions. Everything is true, the good and the bad.

There's only one thing that remains; your reply. I only ask for one thing, that I see you for at least one more time. Hopefully, it will be our "first date".

Otherwise, it will be the very last time we see each other. Whichever the case, I shall accept it.

Σαν της άνοιξης την παπαρούνα Άνθισες,	Like a poppy of the spring you sprang
Και της καρδιάς μου την ασπίδα Ράγισες.	And my heart's stony exterior cracked.
Χάδια τρυφερά και φιλιά ερωτευμένα Πέταξες,	Tender caresses and kisses in love you threw away,
Σ'έναν τάφο στο υγρό χώμα Έθαψες.	In a wet grave you buried them.
Σαν μεθυσμένη από κρασί εύκολα Ξέχασες,	Like drunk on wine easily you forgot
Όσες υποσχέσεις παθιασμένα Έδωσες.	All the promises so passionately you made.
Της λήθης το πηγάδι άνοιξα, Τα φιλιά μου μέσα να πετάξω,	I went to the well of lost memories Therein my kisses to throw
Ώστε να διατηρηθούν ζωντανά Μέσα σ'ενα σκοτάδι αθάνατο.	So they'll remain alive Within the immortal darkness.
Της αγάπης την ελπίδα Φρέσκια μες στην καρδιά κρατώ,	Love's hope Within the heart to keep fresh,
Με όνειρα απ'τον χρόνο σβησμένα Να ζήσω προσπαθώ.	As I try to live With dreams murdered by time.

(written and sent amid a long bender of boozing,
severe drug-abuse, and multiple one-night stands)

All these days and nights, the same questions arise in my head, tormenting me during my reading, my writing, my attempting of living. What went wrong? What is the *real* reason we cannot be together? What is it that scared you away? What is it that makes me love you the one day and hate you the next?

Are the promises to blame? We did give grand promises to one another once; in the beginning, when the enthusiasm was so great, when we let our mutual attraction, the excitement, the still under-development feelings of true affection take over our minds and bodies and dictate our actions. We made grand proclamations to one another, because we believed them, or so we, at least, thought. Were they true? At the time, yes they were. We meant everything we said; we could never honestly admit it, however, because of the situation, of everything else that was outside the tiny bubble wherein we had placed our relationship. The truthfulness of our promises and of our big words could not be admitted, not even to ourselves, because it would endanger everything else; it would destroy the world outside our very own tiny jar.

Was there though *any* truthfulness in our words and promises? Or were we simply swept by the intensity of the moment, that we made believe out of them? Did we simply convince ourselves for a brief time that everything we proclaimed to each other was honest, merely because it was what we both needed? Were our statements frank, coming straight from the heart, or were they nothing more than empty words, a desperate attempt of two cold, loveless souls to experience some much needed warmth? Questioning the truthfulness of all our proclamations is a sharp dagger through the heart, for I have wished for so long to believe all the words your lips have uttered; equally, I fear questioning the honesty of my own feelings and intentions. However, it is, most plausibly, the most important of all questions. For, if we were untrue to each other, if all we did was to seek comfort to each other during a time of need, without actually experiencing any of the emotions we thought had flooded our hearts, then, there is no purpose in our relationship; we were two lost vessels, which found each other in the middle of a vast, dark, dangerous ocean, and we leaned on to each other until we could find a safe harbor to rest. We found the harbor—or, at least, you did—and now, we can go our separate ways, we can remap our routes and never meet again. Was this the purpose of our meeting? To keep each other safe and warm, and alive, during a time of turbulence, only to abandon each other, as soon as the weather grew calmer and safer? Unfortunately, there are no definitive answers; I do not know what is going on in your mind, what your thoughts are, what your true feelings are. I only know the things you tell me; and, for better or for worse, I cannot be certain of the honesty of those words, nor of how much you are concealing from me, for whatever purposes you may have. Similarly, I cannot know the answers from my own side, either; how can I, after all, when I find myself dreaming of you the one night and shedding tears of sorrow for missing you from my bedside, only to wake up the very next morning loathing the very thought of you, the mere idea of you ever being a part of my life? When both the missing and the loathing are equally true sentiments, how can I know what I truly want; how can I say, whether I meant the things I once told you, or if I mean what I say now? Do I really want you back, as I sometimes wish upon the stars? Do I honestly desire to hold you in my arms once again, and to kiss you, and to show you how much you mean to me? Is the wish to tell you to go to Hell, the burning desire to shut you out of my life forever, equally true? I don't know.

Without a shadow of a doubt, the situation shaped the rocky course of our relationship; had we started under healthier, more "normal" circumstances, things would have unfolded much differently. The past cannot be changed, we have to play with the cards dealt to us, hence, there is no reason to brood over things we cannot possibly alter, nor influence. On the other hand, we *can*, and should, acknowledge the role the situation played, its influence to our little story. It was, after all, the situation that created a lot of the difficulties we faced, and which caused the ups and downs, the very highs and very lows through which we've been. The intense beginning, the emotional middle, the harsh first ending, they were all caused by the situation. It was an impossible situation, hope was not there to begin with, yet we created hope, because we both needed it. It directed us between a rock and a hard place, and we paid the price of being in the middle. It made us love each other, it forced us to hate each other. We said goodbye, because it could not go on, we were poisoning each other, we were destroying each other's life; the parts of our lives that were left outside our personal jar.

Yet, we could not live without each other; why? We had bonded too strongly in such a short time, so that when time came to leave each other in peace, we left a hole in each other that could not be filled in any other way. You sought me out, I welcomed you back. We had both dreamt of each other, and of us being together, that the dream had become too strong to be killed; we lived out our little fantasy, we spent a few weeks living the dream. It felt good, it felt right; the circumstances also allowed it to happen. Suddenly, things changed again. Why?

You had a new beginning ahead of you, an uncertain future. However, you suddenly felt you didn't want me into this new future. You wanted independency, freedom; you had dreamt of me, when you didn't have your freedom, and you had wished I was around. Suddenly, you were liberated of all constraints, you were able to live a life you didn't know, and I was no longer needed. You killed your dream easier this time, because you had found a different dream. We both wanted to experience something new—the issue is, what is new to one, is old to the other. You dream of the life I once had, I desire the life from which you only recently escaped.

Can we overcome this issue, our different aspirations? Is it even realistic to believe that there is a chance for us to arrive to a feasible solution, which would allow the hope of what we once wished to come true? I fear I do not know. Sometimes, I hope there is a solution, which I cannot, for the time being, see. There are times, though, where I feel certain there is no such solution, but one; the waiting. Perhaps, if we wait long enough, we'll realize how much we mean to each other, and it will help us put aside all the differences, the dreams we've killed, the hate we've created, the mistakes we've committed. How long will this waiting last? And is it worth it?

Naturally, there is only one real answer to these questions: only time will tell. A most general, vague, abstract answer, to questions demanding a more specific answer. Henceforth, is there anything that can be done to salvage what is left from something that once was beautiful? Of course, a mutual desire to preserve the beautiful and fight the ugly, in order to maintain the hope of the future alive is the first, and most vital, requirement. The fear of commitment is understandable; we both need time, we both need to take it slow. If we jump onto the bandwagon too quick, we'll lose our balance, fall and kill the hope, which is already hanging from a thin threat. Hence, taking it slow is the only way. Is it possible?

Are we capable of putting whatever we have dreamt and wished aside, for the sake of a prospect? Can dreams—that were once so beautiful and heartwarming—be killed, or, at the very least, be put aside? Or, are they bound to haunt us forever, thus not allowing us to do what we ought, and ultimately destroy the traces of hope that remain?

Again, only time will tell. We can search in ourselves as much as we want, we can spend as much time as we want apart, we can perform as many soul-searching journeys as we can withstand. No definitive answer will arrive in our minds, and hearts. We'll still miss each other, because we once came to mean so much to each other, the dreams will persevere dearly in our subconscious. We'll still shed a tear, whenever we realize how we killed our dream, how we never gave it a real shot, because we were afraid. However, when we are together, bad blood ensues; we remember the difficulties we've been through, the serious discussions, the harsh words, the heated moments. The times where care was replaced with despise, love with hate. And we can't be around each other; we remind each other things we wish not to remember.

I am the great mistake you almost committed, you are the reason I almost changed my entire being. Sacrifices too grand we underwent, because the promises were equally important. The situation killed any chance we might have had to discover if the changes, the sacrifices, the promises, were worth it. We couldn't discover firsthand if it could have been as great as promised, or if it would have been the nightmarish failure we feared. We stayed on words, on speculations. It led us nowhere; perhaps, it saved us some heartbreak. Nonetheless, we had our fair share of heartbreak, a little more wouldn't have been enough to kill us. At the last moment, we got scared, we backed down; we saw the dream slowly coming to life, and we put a knife through it, sent it back to the world of Morpheus, whence it came.

Consequently, what is going to happen? Is there still any trace of hope? Do we both share the same dream, no matter how impossible it may seem? Do we still possess the desire we once shared? The passion, the affection? Or were all the big words, the strong emotions, the promises, products of the heat of the moment? Were we simply so caught up at our need to escape that we made each other believe and hope, without really wanting to? Or did we just get too scared, when we saw the dream suddenly becoming possible? Was it only the lack of hope that allowed us to dream? When we thought it'd never happen, we nearly committed to the realization of the dream, despite comprehending it was condemned to a gruesome death. Suddenly, when it actually materialized, when it received a prospect of becoming true, we backed away. Was it thus only the hope we were looking for, the comfort found only in unfulfilled dreams and in secret, sinister thoughts?

The future holds no guarantees; we are now living our separate lives, we stay away from each other, in our attempt to think, to kill the dream, to forget everything that happened. Maybe, one day we'll run to each other, because we'll stop fearing and start hoping. At the same time, we may never see each other again, but in dreams. Perhaps, we'll store our memories in our subconscious, bury them deep down in the abyss of our mind, and start afresh, a new life; we'll only recall each other in times of need, whenever we feel lonely, insecure, afraid. When it's cold, the memories will return to warm the heart, then they'll vanish hastily once again, return to the darkest corners of the memory bank, hidden from the light and the world.

We are but two characters in a novel; the great Writer in the sky, the one that decides our fate is typing the last words, the final paragraph. Soon, he'll type "THE END" and the novel will be finished, as will our love. Unluckily, we are the creations of a realist; a man, who does not believe in *happily ever after*. We didn't ask for it, but it's what we were dealt. Let us thus embrace the moments he allowed us to enjoy, and let us not shed any more tears for what we've lost, for what we could have been, had our writer been a romantic. The lemons we were given were sour, thus our lemonade would not be sweetened, regardless of how much sugar we added.

As the night fell upon the city like a dark, unsettling veil, they sat by their windows and stared at the sky and the slowly emerging stars. Unknowingly, they shared one last moment of true affection, when they both shed a single, meaningful tear for their memories. They thought of each other, and felt warmth in their hearts, when the affectionate thought of the other reached their heart. One final metaphysical moment was all they got; the last crooked smile was smiled.

As if coordinated by a powerful puppeteer, they both got up at the same time and returned to their new lives, separated from each other forever. Their love might have been strong, but their differences were stronger, and so, they'd have to look for someone new, to replace what they lost.

THE END

03/03/2016
(written and sent in the mid of a ferocious bender of vices)

Once again, I'm writing for you, and to you.

It feels stupid, insane, asinine, moronic.

It's been, after all, a fucking year since I saw you, since your smile caused my heart to skip a beat.

I've finally realized that you, and everything that happened between us, was a result of you reminding me of someone else; someone I lost due to the drink (and the heavy drug abuses you never got to hear about).

I feel awful. I'm back on the wine; I'm still clean on the drugs. Only an occasional joint, and the every now and then snort of blow. All my connections are gone; I have to cook my own meth nowadays, risking to blow the whole dorm up every Sunday morning (there's a funny story behind it; one of the many you didn't get to hear).

I miss you; that's the worst part. I was in Greece this past Christmas, and if it wasn't for my best friend, who took my phone away when I began drinking too much, I would have texted you through facebook. Now, I'm all alone, in the apartment you probably still remember all too clearly. Wasting my days writing and drinking. There's nothing left to do, and it feels all right.

Soon, I'll wake up in skid row, I'll be sleeping under blankets made of snow, and it feels right; it's where I've always wanted to be.

I'm drunk; I saw your pictures on facebook. They reminded me of your smile, of your body, of your touch. They reminded me of the moments we spent together, even if they were limited, precious, wrong. Because of me, you destroyed what you knew; because of me, you endangered your present and future. Thank you for that.

I did waste ten months of living solely for you; because you reminded me of someone else. Because in your eyes I saw the glance I lost years ago. It sounds harsh, it's true. I've hated you for quite a while; I wished I hadn't met you. Even now, I wish I hadn't met you. The only reason I'm writing this, is that I'm drunk; and drunk words are sober thoughts. Hence, do I still miss you? Do I still wish you were sleeping on my bed, as you did almost a year ago?

I don't know. I don't care to know. You're nothing more than yet another whispering ghost; one of the hundreds that had laid upon my bed. Nevertheless, there was something special about you; looking at your pictures on facebook reminded me of that bizarre uniqueness.

It's been what? 10-11 months since I last saw you? I miss you. I'm back in my old ways; all the old habits have come back. I drink, I smoke, I inject, I snort. Namely, all the things you wished I never did. And yet, even when I write stories about my past (the past before I met you), I still think of you. I'm back, and the old habits have returned too, yet, sometimes, I wish you were still around to prevent me from falling straight down into the deepest infernal pits.

You're not around, maybe it's for the best, and sometimes I miss your touch, your smile, your kiss more than I miss the junk and the ice. Despite the sins, the wrongdoings, I wish you would have given us a fair chance. You didn't, and I understand why.

I write this, after drinking 2 liters of wine. I smoked pot, ate acid, snorted coke, injected junk. All the bad habits are back, and 90% of the time, I'm glad you're not around. Someone else is sitting on the blue, stained couch; someone else is naked on my bed. You're nowhere to be found, and I'm glad that you never existed. And yet, there's still a small, yet precious, amount of time, where my mind remembers you and my heart wishes to see you again.

Just to see you knocking on my door again, even if it meant I'd have to hide the bags of junk, glass, and blow. Sometimes, I long for another warm embrace, a loving kiss, an affectionate night. You're away, and I'm back to having nameless one-night stands with model-esque blondes, whose names I cannot remember after the first junk injection.

Are you still out there?

Will you reply to this text, or are you completely over me?

It doesn't matter.

My drunk heart said, "send it", and I did.

I had to drink, to snort, to inject.

And yet, despite the drugs poisoning my blood

I still fucking love you.

Isn't that pathetic?

another sip of wine,

your smile is stronger,

Prevails over the rest of the whispering ghosts.
you won't reply;
you won't give a fuck;
you'll read the lines and erase them;
you found a new embrace wherein you find
safety and comfort;
I don't give a fuck anymore.
I just had to let you know
I still remember you,
despite the harsh words exchanged,
despite the way we ended an affair
that was meant to end in nothingness.
I'm still here,
you're still there.
It's all that matters.
Whatever we shared,
it's insignificant.
We are still here,
I still think of you;
do you still think of me?
That's the only question worth asking,
the only line worth the words
deriving from a bruised heart
and a beaten liver.

George Gad Economou, born in 1990 in Athens, Greece, has a Master's in Philosophy of Science from Aarhus University and is currently residing in Athens, working as a freelance writer. His stories have appeared in various online outlets, such as Spillwords and Jumbelbook.

Thank you to the Wapshott Press sponsors, supporters, and Friends of the Wapshott Press.

Kit Ramage
Muna Deriane
James Wilson
Rachel Livingston
Kathleen Warner
Robert Earle and Mary Azoy
Kathleen Bonagofsky
Suzanne Siegel
Phil Temples
James and Rebecca White
Richard Whittaker
Debbie Jones and Steven Acker
Cynthia Henderson
Nancy Lilly
Jennifer Bentson
Patricia Nerad
Ann Siemens
Elaine Padilla
Laurel Sutton
John Grigor Bell

The Wapshott Press is a 501(c)(3) not-for-profit enterprise publishing work by emerging and established authors and artists. We publish books that should be published. We are very grateful to the people who believe in our plans and goals, as well as our hopes and dreams. Our new website is at www.WapshottPress.org. Donations gratefully accepted at www.Donate.WapshottPress.org.

www.ingramcontent.com/pod-product-compliance
Lightning Source LLC
Chambersburg PA
CBHW070538130626
46555CB00003B/1481